To Barbara McNally

—*Gloria*

To Isabel, Max, Jackson, and Hunter

—*Yan*

Text Copyright © 2008 Gloria Whelan
Illustration Copyright © 2008 Yan Nascimbene

Sleeping Bear Press™

310 North Main Street, Suite 300
Chelsea, MI 48118
www.sleepingbearpress.com

© 2008 Sleeping Bear Press is an imprint of Gale, a part of Cengage Learning.

Printed and bound in China.

10 9 8 7 6 5 4 3 2 1

ISBN: 978-1-58536-352-0
Library of Congress publication data on file.

YUKI

and the ONE THOUSAND CARRIERS

GLORIA WHELAN

Illustrated by YAN NASCIMBENE

Tales of the World *from* Sleeping Bear Press

ANCIENT JAPAN

AUTHOR'S NOTE

I was inspired to write *Yuki and the One Thousand Carriers* after seeing an exhibition of woodcuts by the nineteenth-century Japanese artist Utagawa Hiroshige. The exhibition at the University of Michigan Museum of Art was of Hiroshige's series "The Fifty-three Stations of the Tokaido Road."

In the seventeenth and eighteenth centuries the provincial governors of Japan were required by law to spend half of their time in Kyoto, the home of the emperor and the imperial court, and half of their time in Edo (today's Tokyo), Japan's political center, ruled by the shogun. The 300-mile road between Kyoto and Edo went over mountains and along the sea.

I longed to take that journey into a distant time and far country. I sent Yuki in my place.

—*Gloria*

"Yuki, come at once," Mother says. "Your father has been called to Edo by the noble shogun who watches over our country. We must prepare for a long journey. Take all you need. One thousand men go with us to carry our baskets and chests."

I do not want to go, but it would be disrespectful to say so.

My honorable teacher throws up her hands. "Such a journey will take many weeks. What of your lessons? Each day you must write a *haiku*. And Yuki, do not forget me."

I pack twenty of my favorite umbrellas, fifty of my best kimonos, and all my fans. I take brushes and ink and many sheets of rice paper for the *haiku*.

I tuck my little dog, Kita, into the basket that holds my sashes.

Mother and I climb into our *palanquin*,

the wooden box that we will ride in. There are cushions of silk to sit upon and a silk cushion for Kita as well. There are wooden shutters so we can see out, but no one can gaze in at us. Six carriers lift the *palanquin* on their

shoulders and we set out.

When we come to the gate, the guards open it, bow low, and let us pass.

I write my first *haiku*.

> ***Once outside the gate***
> ***how will I find my way back?***
> ***Will home disappear?***

The shouters run ahead crying out,
"Lie down! Lie down, in the dust."
All must bow to us for Father is the
governor of our province.

After the shouters come the samurai
with their fierce looks and then Father
wearing a robe embroidered in gold.
I can hear the bells on his horse. Finally
it is our turn. The carriers are last, their
backs bent low under their burdens.

We are a dragon
Our one thousand carriers
the dragon's long tail.

Rain begins to fall.

The round hats of the carriers are like
umbrellas. I put my hand out to feel the
warm spring shower. Kita licks my wet
hand.

Rain coaxes flowers
pear blossoms will soon bloom here
I will not see them.

The sun hides behind the hills.
It is finished with our day. The road
disappears in the dark until the
torches of the carriers bring it back.

"*Okaasan*," I ask Mother, "when will
we eat? Where will we sleep?"

"Peek through the shutters,"
Mother says.

In the breeze the lanterns of an inn
wave at me. "Before our journey is over,"
Mother tells me, "we will have stayed at
53 inns."

For many long nights
my bed at home lies empty
just waiting for me.

Mother and I share an eight-mat room.

Here is what I eat: bean curd soup, sushi,
shrimp, dumplings, pickled ginger, and
carp. Kita eats everything but the ginger.
I am asleep before the oil in the lamp is
all gone.

With a full stomach
even the wooden pillow
holds my head softly.

We come to a river, a blue ribbon we
have to cross.

The horses plunge into the water.
The carriers take off their kimonos
and bundle them on their heads.
Our *palanquin* is placed on a raft and
ten carriers wade it across the river.
Not even my toes get wet.

> *River is busy*
> *making its own long journey;*
> *it doesn't look back.*

At last night's inn the shampoo lady
washed my mother's hair, then she
washed mine and rolled it into a big
puff. My hair is stuck with so many
hairpins I feel like a porcupine.

This morning our path follows the river.
The carriers sing songs as they travel.
They bathe their tired feet and splash
in the water to cool themselves. Trees
march along the bank with us.

Willows lean over
the river's edge like women
washing their long hair.

Today the path climbs up the side of the mountain. I hear the carriers groan, for our *palanquin* is heavy on their shoulders.

>***At the mountain top***
>***I see my father on his horse***
>***far away from me.***

The path clings to the mountain's edge.

"*Okaasan*," I ask, "will we fall off?"

"No, no," Mother says, "thousands have gone safely before us and thousands will come after."

>***Narrow mountain path***
>***is a strong hand that holds us***
>***won't let us turn back.***

A white surprise! The snow forgot it
was spring.

The carriers tread carefully on the
slippery path. I feed snowflakes to Kita.

> *Snow on the treetops*
> *snow on the carriers' hats*
> *snow hides the way home.*

A fox trots through the woods.

Mother tells me a fox is cunning and can
change itself into a man, but it cannot
lose its tail. I think that would be a
funny looking man. Kita growls and
Mother says a dog can see through the
fox's trick.

> *I would change into*
> *a bird, fly out the window*
> *soon I would be home.*

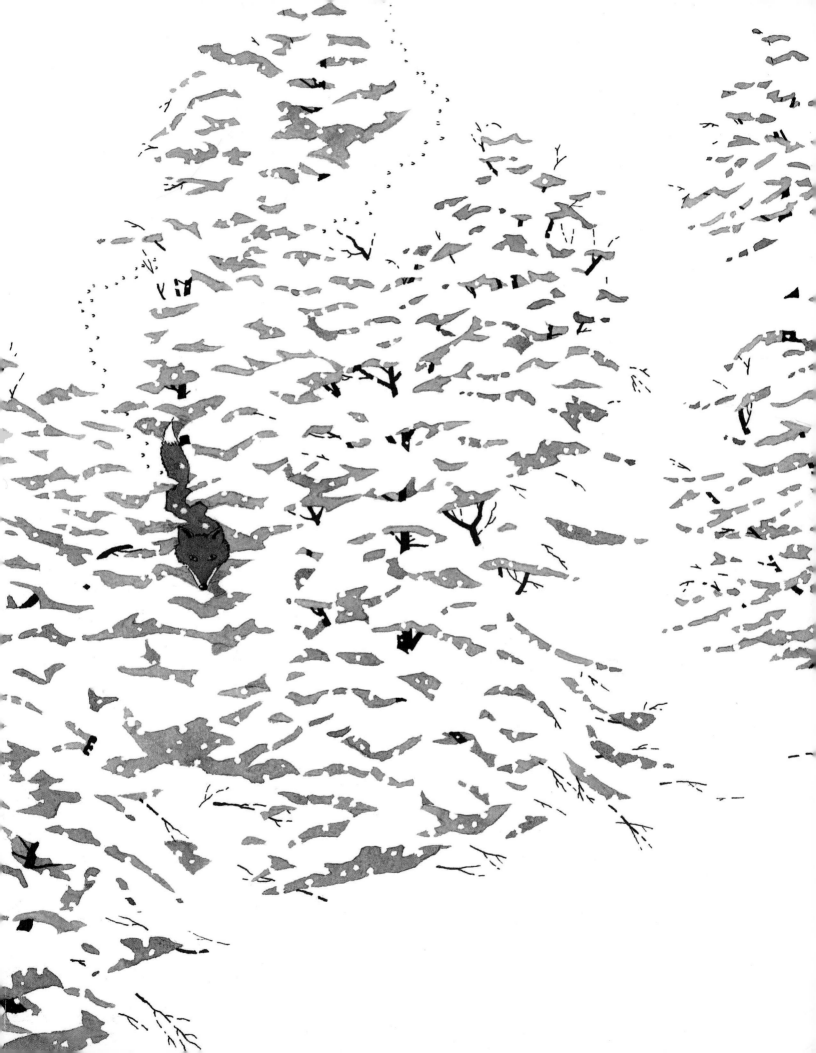

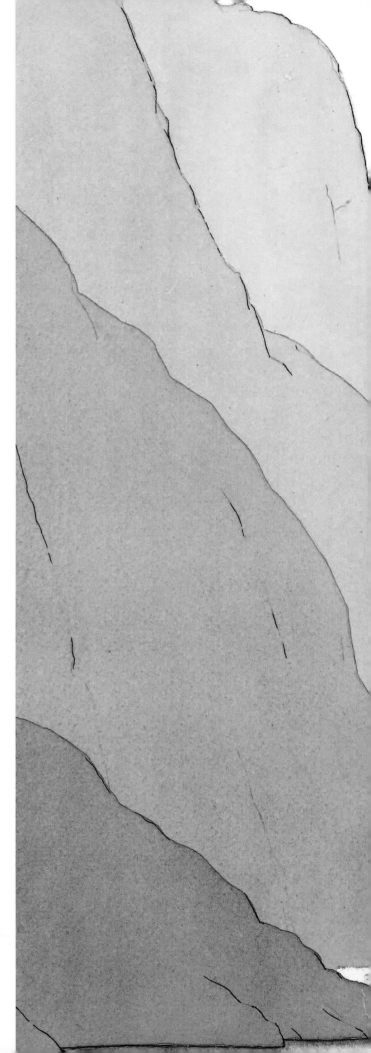

Tucked into the mountain is a village of little houses. They huddle together like good friends. Smoke rises from their cooking fires. On the clotheslines brightly colored kimonos flap in the breeze.

I see the children
happily playing at games
their homes close by.

Our inn tonight is in the village of Middletown. We are halfway between Kyoto where our honored emperor lives and the shogun's palace in Edo.

Our room in the inn is only a five-mat room. Worse, our bedclothes are dirty. Mother gives the innkeeper such a scolding he runs from the room with his hands over his ears, Kita chasing after him.

Today the way home
as close as the way to Edo,
tomorrow, further.

At the bottom of the mountain is the sea.

Fishing boats with their white wings
sail into the harbor like a flock of gulls.
The moon climbs the sky.

> *Fishermen at sea*
> *follow the moon's golden path*
> *return safely home.*

There are many fishermen in this town.
For our dinner tonight we have broiled
eel, shark, and octopus. In the morning
when a rooster awakens me I see all the
fishing boats have disappeared.

> *Gulls write their haiku*
> *in the sky, dipping and darting*
> *not caged in a box.*

When we come to Suruga Bay we have our first glimpse of Mt. Fuji.

Fuji stretches so high it pushes through the clouds. The top of the mountain is covered with snow. Fuji is a sacred mountain where spirits live. In the spring they come down to help the rice grow. In the fall they go back to the mountain.

Mother says women and girls are not allowed on the mountain.

When the darkness comes
and the spirits are fast asleep
Yuki will climb Fuji.

I am tired of riding inside the *palanquin*.
I beg, "*Okaasan*, let me walk a little way."

She looks about, to be sure there are no
strangers on the path. "Only for a very
short distance," she says, "and do not
stray, Yuki."

I think she would like to come with me
but it would not be seemly for the wife
of a ruler.

I bring my basket with Kita. The carriers
tease me. They say, "Now you are a carrier,
too." Kita squirms to get out of the
basket. When I let him out he dances
with happiness.

Soon we are back inside the box.

> ***Grass under my feet***
> ***plum blossoms drift down on me***
> ***just for a minute.***

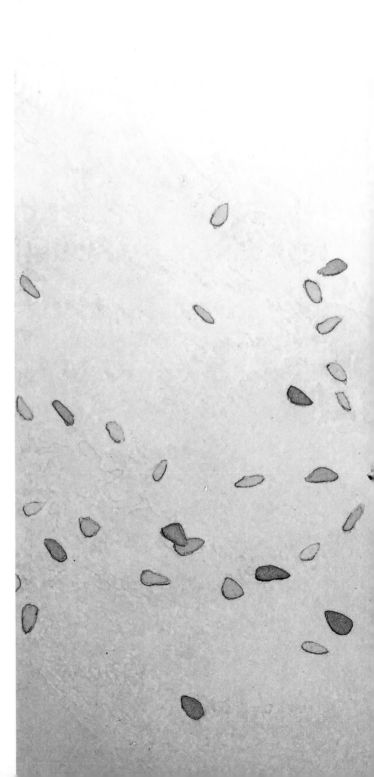

The carriers shout with excitement.

Mother and I peek out. There is the great city of Edo. We cross Nihonbashi Bridge, the point from which all distances in Japan are measured.

A path goes two ways
I have traveled one way, when
will I travel back?

There are many people. There are more houses than I can count. Kita barks at a city dog. I cling to Mother so that she does not lose me. Our procession stops at Edo Castle where the shogun lives.

Before Father enters the castle he turns and smiles at me to let me know I have been with him on the journey.

I say *sayonara* to our one thousand carriers.

Everywhere I see
something to delight my eyes
I stop looking back.

※